Sammy S Big Golf Tourney

tate publishing
CHILDREN'S DIVISION

By Coach Sloth

Published by Tate Publishing & Enterprises, LLC
127 E. Trade Center Terrace | Mustang, Oklahoma 73064 USA
1.888.361.9473 | www.tatepublishing.com

Tate Publishing is committed to excellence in the publishing industry. The company reflects the philosophy established by the founders, based on Psalm 68:11,
"The Lord gave the word and great was the company of those who published it."

Book design copyright © 2011 by Tate Publishing, LLC. All rights reserved.
Cover and Interior design by Stan Perl
Illustration by Kurt Jones

Published in the United States of America

ISBN: 978-1-61346-738-1
Juvenile Fiction / Sports & Recreation / General
11.08.19

DEDICATION

**To my daughter Taylor & my son Tucker.
"Believe to Achieve!"**

ALSO BY COACH SLOTH

Sammy Sloth: Sport Superstar
Sammy Sloth is on a quest to become a sport superstar! Unfortunately, after trying out for the track, baseball, and swimming teams at school, Sammy still hasn't found his sport. Is there any sport out there that will fit his slow and steady nature and allow him to become *Sammy Sloth: Sport Superstar?*

Sammy Sloth   Walter Walrus

Good morning, golf fans! This is Murph Moose alongside Andy Aardvark and greenside reporter Joe Jackal. We are coming to you live from the Belmond Country Club, host of this year's Animal Masters Golf Tournament. Today's pairing features youngster Sammy Sloth against long-ball hitter Walter Walrus.

"Walter Walrus is a good golfer," says Sammy Sloth. "There is no way I can beat him."

"Always think positive and have confidence," says Tucker Turtle. "Believe you can win!"

Sammy Sloth hits good golf shot after good golf shot to beat Walter Walrus and advance to the next round against the fierce Shaun Shark.

"Shaun Shark is a really good golfer," says Sammy Sloth. "There is no way I can beat him."

"Always think positive and have confidence," says Tucker Turtle. "Believe you can win!"

Great golf shot by Shaun Shark from deep in the water, but not quite good enough to beat Sammy Sloth.

Day two is over, and Sammy Sloth advances to round three against legendary golfer Gerrick Golden Bear.

"Gerrick Golden Bear is a great golfer," says Sammy Sloth. "There is no way I can beat him."

"Always think positive and have confidence," says Tucker Turtle. "Believe you can win!"

Gerrick Golden Bear sinks a long putt, but Sammy Sloth answers right back to advance to the championship round against the mighty Taylor Tiger.

What do you think, Andy? Does this young sloth have what it takes to tackle the world's number one player?

We'll see, Murph, but the odds are certainly stacked against him.

"Taylor Tiger is the best golfer in the world," says Sammy Sloth. "There is no way I can win the tournament."

"Sammy, always believe you can win!" demands Tucker Turtle. "You must think positive and have confidence."

We are on the eighteenth hole, and surprisingly Sammy Sloth
is tied with Taylor Tiger. Let's find out who is going to win the
championship. Sammy Sloth smacks the tee shot down the
middle while Taylor Tiger slices the shot into the woods.
Somehow Taylor Tiger finds the ball and hits an amazing
shot off a tree and lands on the green just inches from the
hole. Now the pressure is on Sammy Sloth to come up big.

Sammy Sloth tells Tucker Turtle, "I believe I can make this shot and win!"

Well, boys and girls, it's come down to this final shot, says Murph Moose. *Sammy Sloth takes his slow and steady swing and hits the ball high in the sky. The ball is right on target as it lands on the green and starts to roll toward the hole.*

I think it has a chance to go in! yells Andy Aardvark.

Look at this! Look at this! It might be, it might be ... YES, it's in! Unbelievable! The crowd is going wild as Sammy Sloth just made the shot of the century to win the Animal Masters Golf Tournament!

"Sammy Sloth *meeeans* business!" exclaims greenside reporter Joe Jackal. He asks champion Sammy Sloth, "What advice would you give to become a champion?"

"To become a champion you must practice, work hard, think positive, and have confidence to win!" replies Sammy Sloth.

There you have it, kids, words from a champion. Thanks for joining us as we just witnessed Sammy Sloth show the confidence needed to pull off an incredible upset.

e|LIVE

listen|imagine|view|experience

AUDIO BOOK DOWNLOAD INCLUDED WITH THIS BOOK!

In your hands you hold a complete digital entertainment package. Besides purchasing the paper version of this book, this book includes a free download of the audio version of this book. Simply use the code listed below when visiting our website. Once downloaded to your computer, you can listen to the book through your computer's speakers, burn it to an audio CD or save the file to your portable music device (such as Apple's popular iPod) and listen on the go!

How to get your free audio book digital download:

1. Visit www.tatepublishing.com and click on the e|LIVE logo on the home page.
2. Enter the following coupon code:
   ded1-03d8-aaad-4c5e-27fc-52bd-5867-9dac
3. Download the audio book from your e|LIVE digital locker and begin enjoying your new digital entertainment package today!

CPSIA information can be obtained at www.ICGtesting.com
Printed in the USA
LVOW05s0843060915

453021LV00010B/28/P